The Gate Crashers

Pound Puppies
Lovable, Huggable

The Gate Crashers

by Dennis Fertig
illustrated by Pat Paris

A GOLDEN BOOK • NEW YORK
Western Publishing Company, Inc., Racine, Wisconsin 53404

It was late night at the Pound and everyone was asleep... well, not everyone. Deep in the secret headquarters of the Pound Puppies, plans were being made.

"So, Violet," Cooler was saying to a visiting friend, "this new boarding school is a place where kids live and go to school."

"Yes," said Violet Vanderfeller, smiling. "And the nice people who run it know that puppies are good friends for children."

"Hmmm. Puppies in a school. That's a smart idea!" exclaimed Cooler. "Scrounger, let's sneak some puppies out of the Pound and take them to the school."

Scrounger was about to say "Sure, boss," when The Nose burst into the room carrying a newspaper.

"Have you heard the news?" exclaimed The Nose. "The Mayor has fired Dabney Nabbit and hired a tough new dogcatcher. Nabbit is packing his things right now!"

Cooler knew that as long as Nabbit was dogcatcher, he and his friends could use their secret tunnels to escape the Pound and help other puppies find homes. No new dogcatcher would be as easy to fool.

"Don't worry," said Scrounger. "Cooler will think of a plan. He always does. He'll save Nabbit's job."

"Yeah," said Cooler, deep in thought. "But this is a tough one, even for me."

As he spoke, Cooler glanced at the newspaper headline: ESCAPED ZOO LION CAPTURED. His eyes lit up.

"Gang, we're going to make the Mayor want to keep Nabbit," stated Cooler. "And we're going to give some puppies a good home at the boarding school. Listen...."

Cooler told the group his plan, and in a few minutes the puppies were busily at work.

Violet and Scrounger had extra special jobs. In one room,
Violet was sewing a costume. It was a lion suit big enough
for two puppies to fit into.

In another room, Scrounger worked on two different projects. First, he hooked up a special telephone and tape recorder in the Pound Puppies' Mission Control Room. Then he sneaked out of the Pound and connected the phone lines to the Mayor's house. Now all the Mayor's phone calls would come to the Pound.

Scrounger's second project was even trickier. Using parts he had found in the trash outside an electronics company, he made a TV camera. It really worked!

Then Scrounger found a picture of a roaring lion and set it up in front of the TV camera.

Finally, on the roof of the Pound, Scrounger put a special machine that could control the Mayor's TV. The Mayor would see a picture of whatever Scrounger's TV camera was pointing at.

By the time everything was ready, it was morning.

The Pound Puppies had a busy day ahead of them. Cooler and Violet tried on the lion suit. "Perfect fit, Violet," said Cooler. "Let's take our practice run."

They walked right past the spot where Dabney Nabbit was cleaning out his office. They made sure he saw them.

Nabbit mumbled to himself. "Puppies in a lion suit… hmmm…. I bet they're planning an escape!

"Well, I don't care if I *am* fired. I'm going to catch those puppies right in the act!"

Back in Pound Puppy headquarters, Cooler and Violet climbed out of the costume.

Violet said, "I hope your plan works, Cooler."

Cooler laughed. "It's going to be a roaring success," he said.

Then Cooler selected the puppies to send to the boarding school.

"OK, pups," he said. "Do well at school...and don't eat anybody's homework!"

That evening the phone rang at the Mayor's house. "Hello," said the Mayor.

"This is Police Chief Williams," said the voice on the phone. "Bad news, Mr. Fist. Another lion has escaped from the zoo. And it's heading your way!"

"My way!" gasped the Mayor.

"Don't worry. My boys will catch that lion," said the Chief, and he hung up.

The Mayor quickly locked all the doors.

At Mission Control, the Pound Puppies had listened to
the phone call and tried not to laugh. The Chief hadn't
really called. It was only a tape recording the Pound Puppies
had made by putting together bits of old tapes of the Chief
talking.

"Swell work," Cooler said. "Now it's our turn, Violet."

They climbed into the lion suit and headed toward the big
gate in front of the Pound.

As usual at night, Itchey and Snitchey were guarding the gate. Cooler and Violet, in the lion suit, crept up to it. When the spotlight shone on them, Cooler roared like a lion.

Itchey looked at Snitchey. Snitchey looked at Itchey. Each one shook his head. That couldn't be a lion—but it was! And those big, mean, tough guard dogs let out little puppy yelps of fear.

The lion roared again and charged at Itchey and Snitchey. The guard dogs took off so fast and so hard that they knocked down the Pound gate. The roaring lion chased right after them.

As soon as the lion raced past the gate, a truck started up.
It was Nabbit's. The dogcatcher had been waiting in the
dark outside the Pound. The truck sped up, and in a
moment, Nabbit had the lion in his headlights. The chase
was on!

No one had seen The Nose sneak away with the Pound Puppies for the boarding school. Within minutes, she delivered them to a bunch of happy kids.

One part of Cooler's plan had already worked.

Meanwhile, Mayor Fist was watching TV and trying not to worry about the escaped lion. Suddenly a news bulletin came on. While a picture of a roaring lion appeared on the screen, a voice announced, "Flash! The lion that escaped from the city zoo has been spotted at 401 Main Street. We urge all citizens to..."

"401 Main Street!" shouted the Mayor, turning off his
TV. "That's *my* address! The lion's *here*!"
    He grabbed the phone and called Police Chief Williams—
or so he thought.

In Mission Control, Scrounger turned off the TV camera. He picked up the ringing phone and set it next to the tape recorder. A voice on the tape said, "Hello, this is Police Chief Williams. I am on an important case right now, but please leave a message after the beep."

Even before the machine could beep, the Mayor's voice could be heard screaming into the phone, "Help, the lion's here!"

And so it was! Cooler and Violet, with Nabbit in hot pursuit, had just reached the Mayor's front porch. They roared and growled. They stomped and scratched at the door. They sounded like the meanest lion that ever was.

"Help! Help!" the Mayor screamed with fright.

Then above the commotion, he heard a voice yelling at the lion. It was someone he knew. It was Nabbit!

The Mayor peeked out a window. He watched in shock as Nabbit grabbed the lion and said, "OK, wise guy. I'm taking you in!"

The Mayor couldn't believe it. Nabbit had saved his life. Nabbit had grabbed that roaring lion and was taking it in! Nabbit was a hero. Nabbit?

Once the lion was safely locked in Nabbit's truck, the
Mayor said, "Nabbit, you're the bravest animal catcher I've
ever seen. You can have your job back."

Nabbit grinned the third biggest grin ever. Cooler and
Violet, in the truck, had the biggest and second biggest grins.

The next day, The Nose came in with the newspaper.

"Listen," she said, "on page three, there's a story about some puppies who have a new home at the boarding school. And on page one, it says the Mayor has announced that Nabbit is getting his job back. The Mayor realized how valuable he is as dogcatcher."

"That's no lie," said Scrounger.

"Of course not," said Cooler, laughing. "We've already had enough *lion* around here!"